SNAP SHOT™

Art director Roger Priddy
Editor Mary Ling
Assistant designer
Joanna Pocock

SNAPSHOT™
is an imprint of Covent Garden Books.
232 Madison Avenue,
New York, New York 10016

Photography copyright © 1991
Jerry Young.
Photography by Dave King, Jane Burton,
Kim Taylor, Steve Shott and Frank Greenaway.
2 4 6 8 10 9 7 5 3 1

Color reproduction by Colourscan
Printed in Belgium by Proost

WILD ANIMALS

Contents

Brown bear

Giraffe

What do pandas munch?

Pandas nibble, all day on a tasty grass called bamboo.

Does a tiger need stripes?

A tiger's striped coat helps it hunt in the grass without being seen.

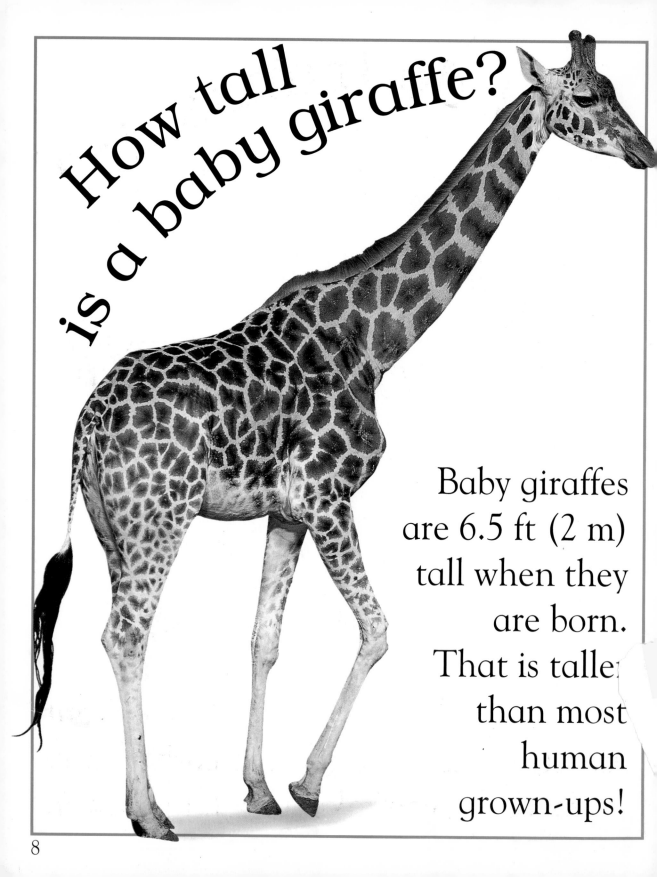

How tall is a baby giraffe?

Baby giraffes are 6.5 ft (2 m) tall when they are born. That is taller than most human grown-ups!

What do trunks do?

An elephant uses its amazing trunk to breathe, carry food, or even take a cooling shower.

What do bears do in winter?

Brown bears sleep all winter.
They dig a den in the ground and
sleep, warm and dry, until spring.

What's in a camel's hump?

Camels keep fat in their humps – like a lunch box, for energy on long walks.

Why do wolves howl?

Wolves howl and growl at one another when competing to be the leader of their pack, or when looking for a mate.

How old am I?

This orangutan is only five years old, but with its shaggy fur and big belly, it is called "Old man of the woods."

Who takes care of me?

A baby gorilla is cared for like a human baby. Mom feeds and nurses it.

Does a 'roo need a tail?

Kangaroos use their tails as props to sit on when they feel like taking a rest.

Smart suit!

Zebras like
to groom one another
to keep their striped suits clean!

How loud is a lion's roar?

A lion roars very loudly to protect his
pride and scare away other cats.
His mighty meow means,
"Beware, I'm angry!"

Can I fly?

A penguin cannot fly.
It uses its flippers
for swimming.
On land, it
hops along
or slides
on its
belly.

What are my quills for?

Porcupines are covered in sharp spikes, called quills. If attacked, it may reverse and give the enemy a prickly surprise!

Do polar bears get cold?

This polar bear has a layer of fat under its thick fur that keeps it warm in cold blizzards.

Can you spot me?

An ocelot's spotted coat helps it
hide in the undergrowth
when it is hunting.

Night hunter!

Panthers hunt at night. Their eyes are six times stronger than human eyes.

What is a rhino's

A rhinocerous has very thick skin that protects it against insect stings, prickly bushes, or even a lion's sharp teeth.

armor made of ?

Who's a clever monkey?

For its
tiny size,
this squirrel
monkey has
a very large brain.

What's so funny?

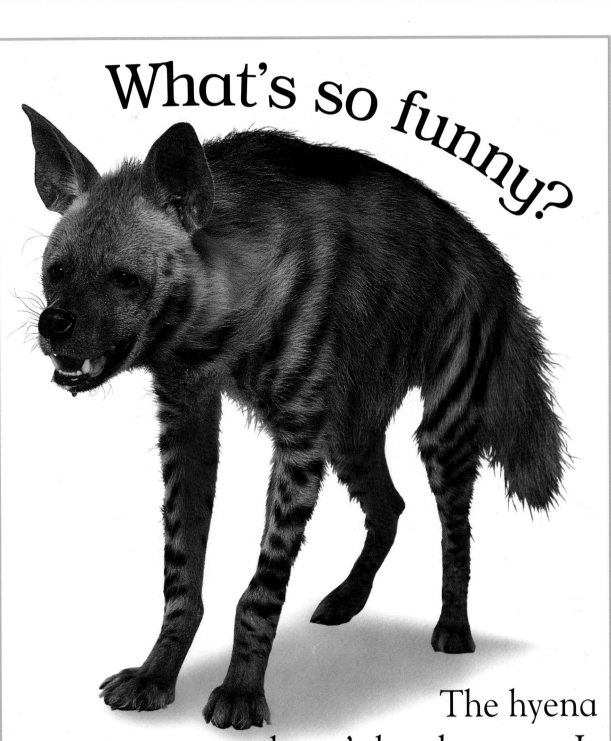

The hyena doesn't howl or roar. It makes a noise that sounds like a laugh.

What a show-off!

Many parrots like to show off their bright colors to attract mates.

Which way is up?

Flamingos dip their strange bills upside down into water and sift the mud, looking for juicy worms and insects.